This book belongs to
the most special flower girl:

_____

The Flower Girl

written by L. Potterton

I feel like a princess in this beautiful dress.
I'm so very excited for what's coming next!

Holding my basket,
I walk down the aisle.

I scatter the flowers, then look back and smile.

My job now is done,
I step to one side.

What a magical moment -
here comes the bride!

There's the groom and the bride,
the vows and the rings.

I can't wait to see
what else this day brings!

The reception starts, the music plays.
The guests all dance in various ways.

This is my favourite sight of them all -
The wedding cake so big and tall.

The stars twinkle,
     the night is clear.

The couple leaves,
     holding each other near.

Their journey together has just begun.
A lifetime of love, laughter and fun.

" I'm so glad I was a part
of your special day! "

I whisper quietly
    as they drive away.

The End